THE BUSY TAILOR CRAB

BY BINGBO
ILLUSTRATED BY GUMI

Mouse
1x trousers
half a day

Chicken
1x t-shirt
1x trousers

Rabbit
1x shirt
1 day

There once was a very famous tailor crab whose job was to make clothes for all the animals.

One day, a praying mantis came to see the tailor crab. "I have a piece of cloth," he said, "but it is a bit small. I cannot figure out what to do with it."

"No problem," said the tailor crab. "Leave it to me. I'll take care of it."

The next day, the crab completed a small waistcoat for the praying mantis. The praying mantis was very happy and gave the crab ten dollars for the work.

Later on, a caterpillar came to see the tailor crab. He also brought a piece of cloth. "I want to wear pants like the others," he said.

"No problem," said the crab. "Leave it to me. I'll take care of it."

The next day, the caterpillar returned, and the tailor crab gave him a pair of pants with six legs.

The caterpillar was very happy

and gave the crab ten dollars for the work.

That night, the tailor crab thought to himself, "The pants I made for frogs and birds had only two legs, but the pants I made for the caterpillar had six legs! I should have charged more money!"

In the morning, the tailor crab posted a notice on his front door. All the animals gathered around to see.

PLEASE NOTE

From now on, I will charge ten dollars for any piece of clothing, regardless of its size, and five dollars for each leg of pants I make.

A small ladybug said, "Oh dear, this is too expensive for me. My body is so small, and I would have to pay too much money!"

That is not my problem," the crab replied. "Regardless of the size of clothes I make, the cost is ten dollars each."

A tiny centipede said, "Oh dear, this is too expensive for me. I have so many legs, and I would have to pay too much money!"

"That is not my problem," said the crab. "Regardless of the size of pants I make, I count the number of legs, and it is five dollars per leg."

BOOM!

BOOM

Next, an elephant came along holding a piece
of cloth on his trunk.

"Hello, can you please make a shirt big enough for me?" the elephant asked.

"No problem," said the crab. "Leave it to me. I'll take care of it."

The tailor crab climbed up and down to measure the elephant for the shirt. At the end, the crab was very tired.

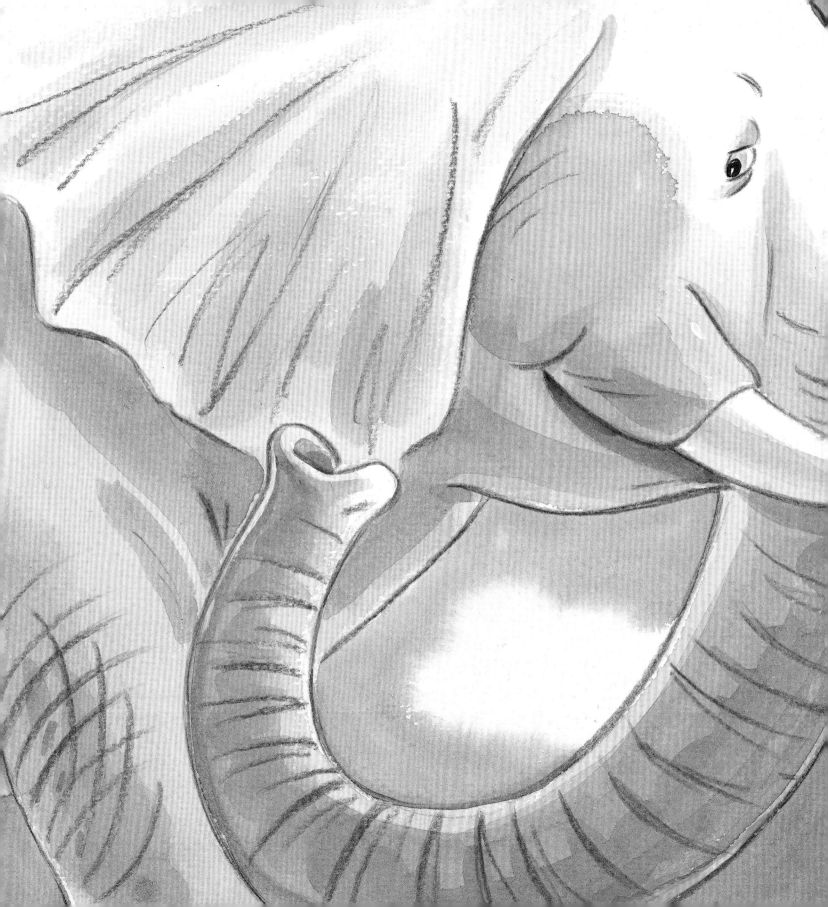

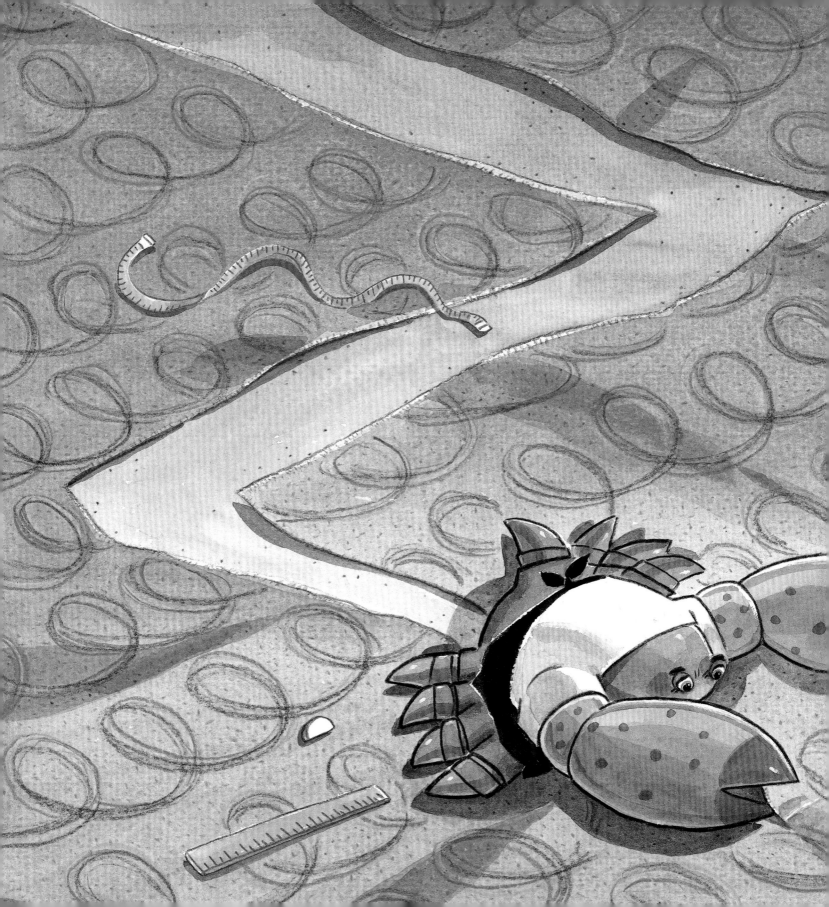

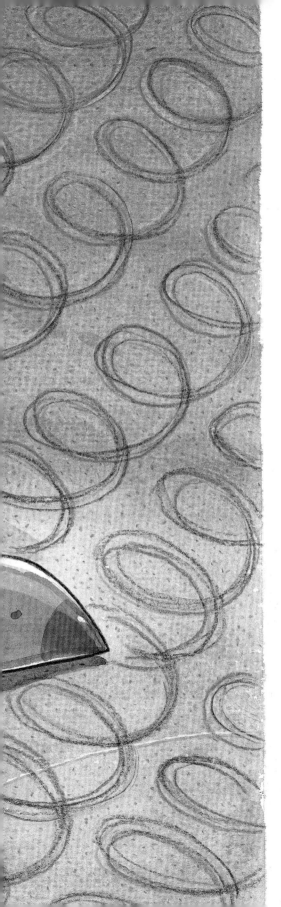

The tailor crab spent the whole night cutting out and stitching the elephant's cloth.

After a week, the elephant's shirt was finally ready.

Elephant
Shirt - 1 piece

Day 1   Day 5
Day 2   Day 6
Day 3
Day 4

The crab said, "It took me so long to make your shirt because it was so big that I won't make any money."

The elephant paid the ten dollars. "That is not my problem," he said. "You said, regardless of the size of the clothes, the cost is ten dollars each."

The next day, a boa constrictor came to see the tailor crab with a piece of cloth folded on her head.

"Hello, can you please make a pair of pants for me? It's getting cold outside, and I want to keep warm."

The crab wondered if the pair of pants the boa constrictor wanted needed to cover her whole body, and he began to sew.

It took the crab three days and three nights to make the boa constrictor's pants.

The boa constrictor was very happy when she put on the pants. "Thank you," she said and turned away.

The crab quickly stopped her. "But you haven't paid for your pants," he said.

"There are no legs in my pants," replied the boa constrictor, "so I don't think I need to pay for these pants. You said five dollars per leg, and these pants have no legs."

"Yes," the crab murmured, "but I spent three days and three nights making the pants... That's not fair..."

When all the animals had gone home, the tailor crab sat all alone and felt very sad. He had worked so hard for so many days and hadn't made much money.

Suddenly, the elephant appeared carrying a big bunch of bananas.

"These bananas are to thank you for making me such a smart shirt."

Then the boa constrictor came along with a big basket of apples on her head.

"This basket of apples is to thank you for giving me such a great pair of pants."

Now the crab felt so happy!

That night, the crab quietly went outside and tore down the notice. "Helping friends makes me truly happy," he said to himself.

Since that day, the tailor crab has lots of customers every day.

www.starfishbaypublishing.com

THE BUSY TAILOR CRAB

Copyright © 2016 by Bingbo and Gumi
First North American edition Published by Starfish Bay Children's Books in 2016
978-1-76036-028-3

原作品名称为《螃蟹小裁缝》（冰波／文，谷米／图）由教育科学出版社于 2015 年出版发行。
此英文版由教育科学出版社授权翻译出版。

PPrinted and bound in China by Beijing Shangtang Print & Packaging Co., Ltd
11 Tengren Road, Niulanshan Town, Shunyi District, Beijing, China
All Rights Reserved.

Chinese author Bingbo has published hundreds of children's stories, winning over fifty awards for his work. These include the Chinese National Award for Outstanding Children's Literature twice, the Soong Ching Ling Children's Literature Award, and the Bing Xin Children's Literature Award. Bingbo has also taught children's literacy in China, whilst continuing to publish his work.

Gumi was born and raised in Chongqing, China. Since graduating from Sichuan Fine Arts Institute, she has worked in advertising and illustration design. Recently, she has focused on illustrating many picture books for children.

Other titles by the same author, Bingbo